Keep the Faith

The Distant Connection

Table of Contents

CHAPTER ONE

Hilton San Diego & Urbanes Headquarters

Monday Morning

"What the hell do you make out of this email Hank sent me on Saturday night?"

Colbert flinched, glad that Harmon wasn't in front of him to see the gesture. "So it's *Hank,* now. Not Bancroft?"

"Just read it. Says he doesn't want to meet with me anymore."

While the line went silent, Harmon got up and went to raid his hotel's mini bar, although it was only 11am. He didn't really care about the clock, anyway, seeing how time didn't care how he felt towards his again-bitter rival.

Colbert read it twice, and then smiled to himself. "What got his hackles up, I wonder?" Secretly he was glad for the tiff, but he'd never say that. The thought did briefly occur to him that maybe one of the photographers Yannick paid off had somehow gotten back to Bancroft, but then he dismissed that fear. It would make no sense, considering they thought the money was coming from him in the first place.

"Hell if I know. He's supposed to meet me for dinner in two days. No idea what caused this total turnaround, and he didn't call me at 10am this morning. I won't tell Stewart, though. Not yet. If you think of anything that could have caused this-"

"I'll let you know, boss. Try to enjoy your vacation in the meantime."

"Yeah. You hear from Yannick again?"

"Not a peep," Colbert lied, having just hung up with him moments before Harmon called.

"Good. Well I'm off to see some damned aircraft carrier or something. You know how my son is crazy about boats. Keep in touch."

"Will do."

Colbert hung up and tried not to laugh out loud. Then he went back to studying the government's many regulations on what exactly constitutes sedition and treason.

Seditionist HQ

Also Monday morning

"Rupe, don't give me a hard time about this one," Hank complained pre-emptively.

"Actually, I was going to agree with you," Rupe responded quietly from his spot in one of Hank's "electric chairs." It always unnerved him to be called in the office like this, but as far as he could tell, he hadn't done anything wrong. Neither had Taylor, who was equally anxious about the reason for this summons.

"Me too, boss," Taylor chimed in. "Changing the emergency number is not a big deal. I say we do it now, especially if someone got a hold of it as you suspected. I see no downside to it."

Hank rubbed his face. "Or maybe it's a moot point altogether, because Daven wants to get rid of all double agents," he blurted suddenly, feeling the rush of irritation surge back up again as he thought about it. "What do you guys think about that? Don't look at each other, look at me. Tell me honestly."

Rupert shook his head. "I don't know offhand. What's his reasoning?"

The fact that Hank didn't know for once what Daven was thinking did absolutely nothing to soothe his increasingly bad temper. "You tell me. You've been talking to him a lot more lately than I have."

Rupe felt his own blood starting to rise, but he would never argue with Hank in front of Taylor. "We didn't talk about that, though. Never even came up. I'm not sure what-"

"What else have you been talking about, exactly?" Hank demanded, and Taylor jumped a little.

"Mostly sports, Hank. And your new house, like everyone else in the neighborhood. It's looking quite formidable in its final stages," Rupert replied easily in an effort to diffuse his boss. Obviously something was bothering him that he didn't want to talk about, and although this mood was rare, everyone knew meetings like this inevitably ended in a nasty fight. Rupert was determined to avoid that at all costs.

Taylor took a deep breath. "Mr. Bancroft, I believe it's because Harmon has claimed he no longer uses double agents. We know Daven doesn't like to look bad in comparison to the

Urbanes, especially after Janet's death. It's only a matter of time before they find out what she was, and they're going to sing it out the world."

Hank looked at her for a moment, his anger put aside as he realized he hadn't exactly been forthcoming with Daven's second-in-command. "They already know, Taylor. I confirmed it some time ago." He looked over at Rupert with a hard expression. "Don't even give me-"

"Hank, how could-"

"*Don't,* " Hank repeated, and Rupe closed his mouth hard. "What done is done, and I've already gotten my ass handed to me about it from Stewart and Daven about it. So just *don't* ."

Taylor looked back and forth between the men. "Then why haven't they made it public yet?"

"Because," Hank replied with a huff, "they're goddamned guilty of her murder, that's why. If I hadn't been banned from talking about it, I would announce it myself."

"Let's not and say we did," Rupert replied after an awkward pause. "Hank, why don't you just tell us what's really bothering you? I assure you we are here to help."

Hank tapped his fingers on the desk and counted to twenty before he responded. "I suspect Harmon is working with a double agent, that's what. One of ours." He looked at Taylor. "And I'm pissed at you for not yet being able to identify who the Urbane was that that I allegedly spoke with before Christmas eve. You had three names, and you can't pin any of them down as suspicious?"

Taylor looked crushed. "No, sir. We talked about this, and how I believe the caller was lying."

"That's not good enough," Hank barked rudely. "Prove it to me. You only have a theory, but nothing to back that up. At least nothing you are willing to stand by for more than thirty seconds at a time!"

Rupert stood up between them as if to physically break the tension. "Alright, let's take a break. Taylor, give us a minute, if you please." He glanced at Hank, daring him to contradict.

Taylor left, and then Hank stood up, too. "You need to go, too."

"Not going to oblige at this particular moment, but I will shortly," Rupe responded calmly as he sat back down. "Your theory on Harmon working with a double agent is important and I want to hear what you have to say about it. Please tell me your thoughts."

That did the trick nicely, and Hank crossed back to his chair with a resigned sigh and picked up a newspaper. "I should have never sent Floyd to that damned boarding school," he admitted bitterly. "Did you see the paper this morning?"

Rupe sat up straighter. "What? No."

Hank's eyes narrowed. "You're the PR guy. It's your goddamn job to be on top of these things before I am."

"You need to calm down," Rupert answered quickly as he reached across the desk to grab the paper that Hank flipped over to him. "You know I was with my son at the doctor this morning and just got here a few minutes ago."

Hank nodded contritely. "Sorry. That was uncalled for."

Rupe took a deep breath and looked at the bottom of page 2. It was a photo of Hank with a private plane - the one that Stewart had forced him to take to and from Philadelphia - and the caption read: *Henderson, Nevada. Hank Bancroft caught wasting his constituent's money on short hops to scout elite private schools for his son, where he was spotted on a joyride to Lake Las Vegas and enjoying a scenic stroll around the lake with his favorite shunned right-hand man, Daven Johansson. One must wonder what the bill looked like for this excursion, and perhaps demand to know who paid for it.*

Rupert took a deep breath. "What the fuck?" he wondered in awe. The media had been unkind to him before, but this was a spectacular new low. "Who the hell wrote this?"

"Anonymous," growled Hank. "But I guarantee you it was goddamned Hailey Hendricks. It gets worse. Read the front page."

On the front of the politics page there was a distant, grainy picture of father and son carrying suitcases under a palm tree, accompanied by a bitter caption: *Hank Bancroft drops his oldest son off Sunday at the most elite and stuffy boarding school on the West Coast, showing his constituents that if you can't solve your problems buying off photographers, you always have other options to throw your money away! Perhaps here young Floyd will learn there are actual, real-life consequences to vandalizing libraries and fighting in church, since his father seems equally as incapable of controlling his sons and his executives when required.*

Rupert was so offended that he didn't know what to say, but Hank had several choice words as he snatched back the paper.

"Fucking Hailey, I'm telling you. And Harmon is orchestrating this. Daven is coming back to work *now* . I'm not waiting until January 26."

"Stewart isn't going to like that," Rupe breathed heavily.

"Fuck him, too." Hank picked up the phone and dialed Dav, who picked up milliseconds before it should have gone to voicemail. "Hey. I need you back to work ASAP. Taylor's not cutting it and shit's hitting the fan. Can you come in tomorrow?...Why not?...I don't give a damn what he thinks, it's my decision. Dav...you know what, come in tomorrow, or don't come in at all ever again. Yes, I'm serious."

He slammed down the phone.

"Hank, stop it," warned Rupert sharply. "We've been through this before. The media will have their fun vilifying you for a few days, and then they'll get bored and move on. You're giving them exactly what they want right now."

Hank threw him a dangerous glare. "I'm telling you, Rupe. Harmon is working with someone on our side, but I don't know who. We need to find out."

"What makes you think that?" asked Rupert angrily. "You haven't said a thing to try to convince me of that, not even one *single* thing. Help me out here."

"I don't know, Rupe," Hank admitted. "I just have a feeling something's rotten in Denmark."

"Quoting Shakespeare, eh? Must be serious, then."

"I am serious. There's something else I need to tell you, and Dav. But you're both going to think I'm out of my mind."

Rupert cocked his head. "I won't, Hank," he replied seriously. "Promise. What is going on?"

Hank reached back to his bar and grabbed a beer as he took deep breaths to calm himself. "It's just that....well, Theo was on the house phone this morning while I was getting ready for work. Calling Floyd to see how he was doing, because he couldn't find his cell phone."

"Okay."

"And he said he heard a strange click."

"....oh."

"Yeah. And when I called Daven just now, I heard the same thing. I've only heard it once before, and that was a few weeks back when Stewart told me that a call between us was being recorded. Rupe, I think my calls are being monitored. Wires tapped. Whatever they call it. Why would that be? They - meaning the FBI - have to find cause for that. Get a warrant, et cetera. They can't just do it willy-nilly."

Rupert let out a low whistle. "Okay, well...how about this, you call me tonight to talk about Theo's first day of homeschooling and you listen for the click. If you hear it again, you might be onto something. For the record, I don't think you're crazy."

Hank laughed without humor. "Well, you have more faith in me than I do at the moment."

"I've always had faith in you, Hank. But to be perfectly honest, that's not going to last long if you don't pull it together and stop losing your shit without much provocation."

Hank eyed him sternly, then put his beer back in the fridge without opening it. "You're telling me to apologize to Taylor, aren't you?"

"Yes. And Dav. And Harmon, but don't hate me for saying that."

Hank grimaced. "I don't hate you. Obviously I owe you an apology as well."

"No, I'm good. Just…for god's sake, be careful about what you say on your landlines from now on. And don't miss any more calls with Harmon."

"Agreed. Thanks, Rupe. I got this. Let's get back to work. Ask Taylor to come in here, please."

FBI Headquarters, Philadelphia

Monday Evening

"Salome, he didn't make his daily call to Harmon today. But if we call him on it, he'll know we're tapping his lines."

"Are you sure?"

"Yes, because Harmon hasn't reported it to me himself."

"That's strange. Maybe he called from his cell phone?" Salome sounded as distracted as she was; stepping into her dress for a date was infinitely more difficult with a cell phone in one hand.

Stewart mulled that over for a while as he doodled in his notebook. "No. Hank's too careful for that. The Seditionists record everything, and he wouldn't want to go off the grid and have a secret conversation, as it were. You know how much he hates taking business calls on his cell."

Salome shrugged. "True, but he's done it before. Ask him about it when you next speak, but don't call him specifically for that. I'm not going to let him get away with disobeying the mandate, period."

Seditionists HQ

Hank stared at his desk phone for another fifteen minutes without moving, then reached for his cell to call Dav.

"Hey, Dav. It's been a hell of a day. I'm headed home. Wondered if you want to come over for dinner with me and Theo."

Daven sat up straighter at his desk, surprised and alarmed. Hank had never invited him over on a Monday night, which had always been his fiercely-protected family evening.

"Everything okay, Hank?"

Hank held back a grimace. "Yeah. Floyd, you probably already know...he's at boarding school."

"Yeah, I read about that."

Groan. "Theo and I could really use the company to distract us from Floyd's absence. Not that you're just a distraction, of course."

"Sure, Hank. What time?"

"In an hour. Chef's already preparing the food. You still vegan?"

"Yes. Don't forget my tofu scramble and kale salad."

That was an in-joke between them; Daven was as carnivorous as anyone could possibly be and barely touched anything that resembled non-meat. Hank smiled briefly, then got serious again.

"You got it. Dav...please forgive me for being a dick this morning. I got my ass handed to me by Rupert about it, and he was right to say I was completely out of line. Those two little blurbs in the paper set me off like you wouldn't believe."

"I believe it, actually. Your boys are supposed to be off-limits."

Hank looked up to see Avery's face hovering behind the glass panel. It was time to go.

"Can you come back tomorrow? Please?"

Daven hesitated. "Did you clear it with Stewart?"

"No."

"Then, no."

Hank sighed. "Fine. I'll call him now. Stay on the line." He had all but forgotten how to conference call, since his assistant always did it for him, but he somehow managed to hit the right combination of buttons and was relieved to hear the phone ringing to his FBI contact.

"Dav, you on the line?"

"Yes."

"Good evening, this is Stewart."

"Sorry to call you so late. This is Hank Bancroft and Daven Johansson."

"Yes, Hank?" Stewart sounded irritated.

"Listen, I want to run something by you real quick. I need to bring Daven back into the office before January 26. Like, tomorrow. A lot going on. Do you see any problem with that, from your point of view I mean?"

There was a slight pause. "Not our jurisdiction at all, but thanks for asking. You may have to answer to your constituents, though. My guess is they'll be really happy he's back and not give you a hard time about it. Glad you called because I have a question for you, actually. Did you have your daily call with Harmon today?"

Hank hesitated, wanting so badly to lie. So much that it physically hurt. "No. There was...no."

Stewart's tone hardened. "You were given a mandate. Do we need to summon you again to drive the point home?"

Hank swallowed hard and flushed, hating being treated like a little boy about to get hauled over a knee, especially with Daven listening in.

"No."

"Call him now so I can honestly tell Salome you two spoke today. She's going to ask me in the morning. Call me back and let me know it's done."

Hank sighed, a little too loudly for Stewart's liking.

"Hank? Would you prefer that I just-"

"No, no, sorry. Will do."

"Good."

He hung up, and Daven breathed out his own sigh. "Jesus, Hank. Are you trying to get yourself-"

"No, I'm not. Listen, are you in for coming back to the office tomorrow, or not?"

"Yes."

"Okay, then I want you on this call with Harmon, and all future ones as well. I'm going to dial him in. Wish me luck."

San Diego

Harmon lifted his head from the pool chaise lounge to peek at his vibrating phone, again. Literally the last person in the world he wanted to speak to, period, was calling him for the third time in a row. He put down his margarita and flipped open the phone angrily.

"I'm on vacation, Hank. What do you want?"

"Uh...Harmon, I'm sorry to bother you. I've got Daven on the line with me, just so you know."

"Okay. I repeat, what do you want?"

Hank cleared his throat and clenched a fist. "Well, since you told Stewart I didn't call you today, I have to call you now and be nice for ten minutes. What are you doing?"

"None of your business, and I didn't tell Stewart anything. Haven't spoken to him in days, and I was perfectly content not hearing your voice today, either."

"Oh." Hank would have looked at Daven quizzically, but he was by himself in his office, so he had to content himself with just staring at his hands. "Sorry for making an assumption. Anyway-"

"Did you tell Daven about that friendly little email you sent me Saturday night?"

Hank swallowed hard, knowing that he was going to hate himself later for groveling to this man. "All about it, actually. Even read it to him. He was appalled, as I'm sure you've guessed. We'd like to come down to San Diego on Wednesday to have dinner with you, if the invite still stands."

"It doesn't. What else would you like to talk about, Hank? Maybe a movie you've seen lately? One you haven't paid for in a cheap motel, that is. Eight minutes left."

Fuck.

"Harmon, this is hardly constructive," Daven responded, and Hank's heart lurched in dismay; he should have instructed the man to keep his mouth shut.

"Uh, Dav, it's alright."

"No, it's not," Daven replied easily. "Harmon, you were right to be angry about the email. We all know that. So that's at least one thing the three of us have agreed upon already. I'm sure there's more where that came from, but we'll never know if we don't talk. You agreed to meet with Hank for a reason, and vice versa. Do you even remember what it was?"

"Of course I do. And it's no longer relevant."

"Why?" asked Daven, genuinely curious.

Dav, I'm going to freakin' kill you where you stand, Hank thought to himself angrily.

Harmon paused. "Because...he obviously doesn't trust me, and I don't trust him. He doesn't even trust *you*. So what's the point?"

Hank broke in now, sweating profusely. "I do trust him, actually. But you're right that I don't trust you, Harmon. I'll tell you exactly why, and what led me to send that email, but only if we meet on Wednesday."

"What's that supposed to mean?" Harmon demanded.

"I mean," replied Hank quickly, "there was a reason I went off on you. A call I received with specific information, probably damaging to both of us, but you'll never know about it if you don't agree to meet. Period."

There was a long pause, and Hank could hear the other two men breathing heavily.

Finally, Harmon responded. "I don't believe you," he replied simply.

"Fine. I'll let Daven say it, then, since you have no reason to distrust him. Dav?"

Slight pause, then Dav's gravelly voice. "He's telling the truth, Harmon. We need to talk. But perhaps not in San Diego, since you're with your family on vacation."

There was another pause, very long this time, and the sound of poolside calypso music invaded the line for about thirty seconds.

"Alright," agreed Harmon, albeit reluctantly. "Cafe La Maze at 6:30pm this Wednesday. It's a private room on the third floor. Come without your guards."

"No. My guards follow me everywhere except the bathroom," Hank retorted. "And sometimes even then."

"Of course. I meant no guards in the room while we're meeting," Harmon amended. "I don't talk in front of servers, either. Period."

"Neither do I," said Hank. "No problem. See you then. And I'll ask Stewart if we can cancel our calls for this week. He probably doesn't know you're on vacation."

"Okay, thanks. See you guys Wednesday."

The noisy line suddenly cut off, and Hank was left on the line with Daven.

"Hank...I'm so sorry. You're going to yell at me, aren't you?" asked Dav in resignation.

"No, actually," Hank replied, and he was surprised to realize that he had forgotten his earlier anger altogether. "You did good, Dav. Really good. Still want to come to my place?"

"Yes. You have to call Stewart back first."

"Ok, I will in a minute." Hank took a deep breath, slightly shaky but calm. He felt emotional suddenly. "Hey, and...thanks for agreeing to come back early. I can't do this job without you. I don't *want* to do this job without you."

Daven swallowed hard. "I wouldn't even want your job at all, Hank. It's a lot. The shit you put up with, and...I'm just really sorry about everything I did to make it harder for you. I hope you'll forgive me someday."

Hank laughed a little, though nothing was even remotely funny at all. "You know me, the world record holder for grudges. But I meant what I said to Harmon. I do trust you. Just...don't give me another reason not to, ever again. Because honestly I won't come back from that a second time."

"Okay," Daven replied quietly. "Deal. I better get up and get dressed."

"You still in your flannel jammies?" Hank asked cheekily.

"They're not flannel, they're...Hank," Daven stopped himself and blushed as he realized he'd honestly answered the teasing question, and now his boss knew he was still in his pajamas after 5pm.

Hank laughed. "It's alright, but I have to admit I'm just a little jealous. Yeah, put on some real clothes, please. See you in about twenty-five minutes."

It felt good to hear Hank laugh, and Daven was pleased, even if it was at his own expense. As usual.

CHAPTER TWO

Hank knew they had made a huge mistake leaving so late in the day for San Diego, and the terrible traffic confirmed his worst fears. They would probably be late for the dinner with Harmon...no, strike that. They would *absolutely* be late. But Hank wasn't willing to call him yet, and he turned to Daven to voice his frustration that the afternoon strategy meeting had gone over by half an hour.

"I told you multiple times to end it, Hank," was Daven's bland reply. As usual, he refused to apologize for something that wasn't his fault. Hank admired that in him immensely, but something in him wanted an apology anyway at times like this. It wasn't fair, and he knew it. So he let it go and fumed silently to himself as they rolled through Dana Point almost an hour later than scheduled. Theo was riding along in the backseat, so there wasn't any opportunity to talk business. Both of them were secretly glad for that, although they wouldn't admit it.

Hank's phone rang with a Palm Springs area code, and his heart lit up like a Christmas tree. He hadn't talked to Floyd yet since dropping him off at the new school, and neither had they exchanged any emails. Even Theo was rather silent on the matter; it almost seemed as if Floyd had temporarily ceased to exist.

"Hank Bancroft," he answered lightly.

"Good afternoon, sir, this is Silas at Elite Palms. I'm your son's headmaster."

"How can I help you?" Hank's heart was now racing instead of glowing. "Is he alright?"

"Yes, sir. Perfectly fine. He got himself into a bit of trouble today, however, and normally I wouldn't bother you with calling for something so minor. But our administrative officer says that you may have neglected to sign the corporal punishment opt-in form, and I just wanted to check that it was intentional. Again, I'm sorry to bother you."

"It's alright, thank you for calling. Is he with you right now?"

"Yes, sir."

"Okay. Please hold for about 3 minutes, okay? Don't hang up."

Hank took a deep breath to calm his nerves, muted his phone, and tapped on the black glass, which immediately rolled down.

"Yes, sir?"

"Vance, I need you to pull over and have Avery follow us. Somewhere private."

"Yes, sir."

Theo tapped his dad on the shoulder, his face twisted in worry. "Everything okay, dad?"

Hank smiled. "Yeah. You know Floyd, probably couldn't keep his big mouth shut. It's fine. I just want to talk to him in private for a minute, okay?"

Two minutes later the cars pulled into the far reaches of a hotel parking lot, and Hank ordered everyone out and into the other car. Once he was alone, he unmuted his phone.

"Silas? I'm sorry about that. Had to, uh, clear the room. Look, I didn't miss the form. Perhaps I should have written *void* on it or something. Sorry about that."

Silas cleared his throat. "Okay, sir, so just want to clarify that you're opting *out* of corporal punishment?"

He sounded surprised, so Hank couldn't resist asking, "Yes. Is that unusual or something?"

"No," Silas replied, "it's becoming less common, but...I only called because your son is the one who thought it was wrong. He seemed certain. Wouldn't accept anything else."

Hank smiled to himself a little. Floyd should have been relieved, but he knew his dad too well.

"I see. Can you put him on the phone, please? I'd like to get the story from him directly."

"Dad," said Floyd a moment later, in a very shaky and fearful tone. "I'm really, really sorry. It was my fault and-"

Hank hardened his tone, although he felt no anger at all. "Floyd, stop. We can exchange greetings first, you know. Haven't spoken in days. Besides this, how are you, son? Liking the school so far?"

"No. Well, not at this moment, but I had been until today," he answered tersely, his tone indicating tremendous levels of stress.

Hank gave up on the greetings attempt. "Okay, just relax. Tell me what happened."

"I ditched class to go back to my room."

"Why?"

"Dad...there was...I had a missed call from Theo, and I was afraid something was wrong with you. I had to call him back right away. I'm sorry. And then..."

"What?"

"Well, I intended to go to class after that, but I got sick. You know what I mean."

The ulcers again. Hank's heart fell to his knees, and anger rose in his throat because this meant Theo was in trouble, too. But that was another story.

"Are you taking your medications?"

"Yes, dad. I'm fine now."

"Put Silas back on the phone."

"Okay, I'm sorry. Here he is."

Hank sighed and tried to phrase his next statement in a way that wouldn't make it sound like the tyrant that he really was on the inside when it came to protecting his sons.

"My son is not getting punished for this, period. He suffers from severe anxiety because of my job, and it leads to issues with his stomach. My other son is at fault here, and I'll deal with him."

"Sir, honestly I did not know that until just this moment. I would have never called you if I knew that."

Now it was Hank's turn to be surprised. "He didn't tell you what was going on?"

"No, sir. He told a...well, a different story than that." Silas sounded horrifically embarrassed, and Hank felt sorry for him suddenly, especially because he had forgotten all about it himself, and there was no way anyone at the school could have known. His anger faded away rapidly.

"I'm sorry," Hank apologized sincerely, hoping he hadn't completely offended the man beyond repair. Then his next words caught in his throat a little as he realized how long it would be before he saw his oldest again. "Let me rephrase and soften what I'm trying to get across. Because of Floyd's, uh, medical issues, I don't want him punished without me being notified *first*. Please call me anytime you need to. You won't be bothering me, I promise. He's my first priority. Can you please put him on the line again?"

"Sure. Here you go."

"Dad, I'm really sorry," Floyd blurted. He was, or had been, crying at some point during this call.

"Calm down and breathe," Hank replied gently. "You tell Silas what you need to tell him, okay? He's there to take care of you, and you need to let him. I'm serious. You understand me?"

"Yes, sir."

"Good. Next time you lie, I'm not going to be opting out of anything. Did you actually talk to Theo?"

Floyd sniffled. "Yes, sir. He just wanted to ask me how I'm doing."

"Okay. We'll talk on Friday night. I have to go. You going to be alright?"

"Yes, sir. Love you, dad."

"Love you, too. Behave yourself."

He hung up and then got out of the car, which caused Avery to leap out of the passenger side of the other SUV to intercept him.

"I need to talk to Theo alone. Send him over, please."

He got back in the car, and a few moments later Theo joined him solemnly. Once the door closed, Hank angrily lit him up.

"Why'd you disobey me, Theody? I specifically told you not to call Floyd during school hours, yet I just learned that not only did you do that, but you managed to panic him and-"

"Dad, stop! I know. I'm sorry." Theo looked about to burst into tears. "I know what I did, please don't yell. Did Floyd get in trouble?"

Hank ignored that. "You and I will be having a chat when we get back to the hotel after dinner. Until then, I don't want to hear another word from you. Nothing whatsoever. Got that?"

Theo nodded, looking completely petrified. "But did Floyd-"

"Quiet. Get in the back row and don't fuss around." Hank got out of the car again, and this time Avery was already waiting a few feet away. "Let's go," he snapped as he caught Daven's eye through the windshield.

They all piled back into the car, and Hank irritably dialed Harmon. He didn't pick up.

"Harmon, it's Hank. Look, I'm really sorry. Had an incident with my son that caused us to stop on the way down, and with traffic like this we're definitely going to be late. I don't think we'll get there until 7:30pm. Call me back. Thanks."

"Everything okay, Hank?" asked Daven very quietly.

"No. Floyd had a freak out and then Theo lied to me, and..." he stopped when he saw the shocked look on Daven's face. "Sorry. Never mind."

"It's okay. You can-"

Hank's phone rang; it was Harmon calling back already. "Sorry, hang on. Yes?"

"Hank, it's no problem. I'll change it to 7:30. Where are you staying?"

"Hilton Torrey Pines."

"Uh....that's where I'm staying. Awkward."

Hank wasn't sure if he should laugh or not, but the remark and teeny-bopper tone was so uncharacteristic that he couldn't help but crack a smile. "Uh, yeah. Guess I should have asked you first. Well, I've got my son with me so I'll need to change it. No offense."

Everyone knew Hank's children were terrified of Harmon. Even Harmon himself. Nothing was worth the risk of running into him.

"None taken. I recommend the Lodge at Torrey Pines up the street. That's where I normally stay on business. It should be available for just tonight. Ask for Brian, he's the evening VIP manager."

Hank found himself blushing hotly, and even squirming under these strange circumstances that had just turned Harmon into his own personal travel agent. "Okay...thanks. I will give them a call."

"No problem. You need to cancel your Hilton reservation though. See you at 7:30."

Hank hung up the phone and the entire car was silent for a long time, because he didn't feel like explaining to Daven what had just happened, even though the man was throwing him curious looks for almost an hour.

Eventually Hank asked, "Vance, how far away are we from the restaurant?"

"About 15 minutes, boss."

"Thanks. Theo?" Hank turned around to look at his subdued youngest son. "Sit up."

"Why are you guys having dinner with Harmon, dad?" Theo responded immediately, his tone angry. He had obviously been wanting to ask the question for a long time, and jumped at the first chance he had.

Hank raised an eyebrow at him while simultaneously berating himself for letting it slip who he had been calling. Damn it. "What have I told you a thousand times before, Theo? Say it."

"Don't ask questions about your work," Theo muttered.

"Thank you. You're going to eat with Vance and the guards because we don't have time to stop at the hotel. While you're waiting for your food, I want you to go into one of the private phone booths and call the Lodge at Torrey Pines and get four rooms with two beds each for tonight under Avery's name. Ask for Brian directly and don't talk to anyone else. I'll give you my credit card. And once you have that done, call the Hilton and cancel our reservations under Avery's name. Okay?"

"Yes, sir." Theo was utterly gloomy, which didn't surprise Hank at all, but he still felt compelled to give the boy something to do to keep his mind off his troubles.

"I'll write down the numbers for you when we get to the restaurant. Then I want you to call Floyd and find out when he's available Friday night for both of us to call him together. Maybe ask him what he wants for his birthday so we can go out shopping for him this weekend."

Theo only became gloomier at that, so Hank gave up the half-hearted attempt to cheer him.

"Also...no dessert or sodas tonight. Only because of the sugar. I can't have you bouncing around the hotel room all night. We're leaving at 5am."

Theo rolled his eyes dramatically. "Oh my *god!* Okay."

Daven grinned sideways Hank, who winked back at him. Then his son laid down again, and the rest of the ride was peaceful.

Palms Elite

After Silas hung up the phone, he turned to his new charge and laid a wary eye on him.

"This could have all been prevented if you had just told me the truth, son."

"I'm not your son," Floyd replied defensively as he wiped away the last of his snot and tears.

"Right, you're not. My apologies. But you are my responsibility for the next five months, and I intend to take your welfare very seriously. Do you need to go to the medical center?"

Floyd shook his head no. "I just want to call my brother."

Silas smiled a little. "Nobody's stopping you, son- er, Floyd. This isn't a prison. Go call him all you want."

"I can't. There are five other people in my room. Can I call him from your office or something?"

"Oh, I see. You want special treatment."

"Yes," Floyd replied defiantly as he raised his chin with pride. "I'm a Bancroft, I can't just be blabbing out family business all over the place."

Silas resisted the urge to laugh. "Floyd, literally every boy here could say the same about their own famous family. You'll have to cope somehow, and I promise you'll survive. Now get going, I have work to do."

Floyd flushed with the grim knowledge that the very first time he ever tried to throw his name around, he failed miserably.

Now he knew why his dad generally refused to do it...it was terribly embarrassing to get shot down in flames like this.

"Mr. Rawson, I'm sorry," Floyd said quietly. Humbly. "I didn't mean to be like that."

"It's okay," Silas said kindly. "Everyone tries that here at least once. Welcome to the club. The only special treatment you're getting is my extra attention to your medical issue, which is more important. I fully expect you not to hide any problems from me again."

"Yes, sir. Goodnight."

"Goodnight, Floyd."

Cafe La Maze, San Diego

In just the last twenty minutes or so, Daven and Hank had grown incredibly nervous about dinner with Harmon, and as they climbed the stairs to the third floor Hank stopped and turned to Dav, lightly placing a hand on his chest to halt his ascent as well.

"I know you already know this, but it's really important that we appear to be completely unified. If you disagree with me on something, keep it under wraps until later. And I'll do the same for you. Agreed?"

"Of course. But Hank…"

"What?"

"Have to admit that I'm really nervous you're going to say something you shouldn't. In fact, I know you're going to. But please don't."

Hank smiled a little. "We talked about this already, remember? I'm going to be a good soldier. But how about this. If I say something you really think is beyond all reason and logic, kick me or something. Grab my leg. Let me know *discreetly* so that I can change tack. Okay? I don't want this to be a disaster for either of us."

Daven frowned. "You want me to communicate my dismay by playing footsie under the table?"

"Yes. We can take it back to my hotel room later if it really turns you on. Now let's go, we're already an hour late."

"For god's sake, Hank," Daven muttered in resignation as he trudged up behind his boss.

CHAPTER THREE

Cafe La Maze, San Diego

Daven hadn't seen Harmon in person in several years, and it appeared to him that the man had not aged one day since then. Or maybe just being on vacation was doing him some serious good. He tried not to stare as Hank shook hands first, and then he quickly lost the staring battle when he was next. His dislike for Harmon had certainly grown by leaps and bounds since then, that much was for certain.

"Daven," cooed Harmon in an overly-friendly manner, "you look much younger in person. But the TV adds years and pounds to all of us, I suppose."

"Nice to see you, too," a visibly insulted Dav snippily answered the backhanded compliment.

Hank butted in quickly before any permanent damage could be done - or at least, he hoped.

"Let's uh, let's sit down and take a look at the menu. I'm starving." He elbowed Dav threateningly, and then threw a wary glance at Harmon's guards, who were staring him down like he had entered the room with a live flamethrower. Avery was doing exactly the same to Harmon, and Hank didn't like it one bit.

"A moment, please," Hank said apologetically as he aborted his attempt to sit down and gestured to Avery, then followed him down the hallway to the edge of the stairs.

"Hey," he whispered sternly. "I really don't like the looks you're giving Harmon. Cut it out and go have dinner."

"I hate this whole situation, Hank," Avery replied in a sullen tone. "Are his guards leaving, too?"

"Yes, and I swear to god if there are is any confrontation whatsoever between you guys, I'll hand down some serious consequences."

Avery looked as hurt as a kicked puppy. "I wouldn't do that, sir."

"I know *you* wouldn't. Not sure about Lucas. These guys are thugs and will absolutely try to start something if given the chance, I've seen it. Don't give in. Warn Lucas and Vance. And even Theo, if you please."

"Yes, sir. But I'm not leaving you alone in this room with them. I'll leave after his guards go first."

Hank took a deep breath. "You'll go now, and-"

"No, sir."

"Avery."

"I said no, sir. Period."

Against his inclination, Hank relented without another word and walked back to the dining room. The man was doing his job exactly as he'd been trained and knew full well he was in the right. And now Dav was throwing eye daggers at Harmon, too. This was going to be a long evening.

"Harmon, I think we can dismiss our guards now," prompted Hank lightly, and the other man nodded and looked at them, pointedly including Avery in his sweeping glance.

"Of course. Gentlemen? You may go."

Avery, of course, would never take an order from Harmon if his life depended on it. He didn't move a single muscle until Hank finally ordered the same, and even then he waited for the other men to go first, holding the curtain aside as they passed through to the stairs. Hank kept a watchful eye on the proceedings and could only finally breathe again once the door had shut without any sounds of a scuffle or argument.

Harmon smiled slightly.

"Don't worry, they've been thoroughly warned to be on their best behavior. Your man seems just as unhappy to be here as mine are."

Hank nodded and sat down, feeling the blood rushing into his limbs again as he picked up his menu. "Well, I guess it's nice to find some common ground right off the bat. Shall we start with a drink or five, gentlemen?"

————

In order to stop the one-sided exchange of murderous looks from his chief of staff to Harmon, Hank had to kick Daven twice under the table before the first round of drinks even arrived. He finally got the message and joined in the small talk, albeit reluctantly and with no enthusiasm. Harmon was showing no signs of aggression whatsoever and seemed to be trying really hard to be agreeable, so Hank quickly became thoroughly embarrassed by Daven's surly behavior.

After they had ordered their appetizers, Hank pushed away from the table and stood up. "Apologies, gentlemen. It was a long drive and we didn't make any pit stops. Please excuse me for a moment. Dav, can you go down and check with Floyd to make sure the hotel reservations are taken care of?"

"Of course," Dav replied quickly, jumping to his feet and hurrying to open the curtain for his boss. He didn't bother to correct him that it was Theo who was downstairs, not Floyd. Hank must really be rattled to mix up his sons like that.

As soon as hit the bottom of the stairs, Hank latched on to Daven's upper arm firmly and all but dragged him into a nearby empty storage room he had noticed earlier.

"Hank, what the-" Daven squeaked in surprise as his boss slammed the door shut and released him.

"*Daven*," Hank growled, using his full name and dragging out the syllables for added emphasis, "if you were one of my sons I'd be taking my belt off right now to correct your manners."

"What?"

"If you can't simmer down and represent us properly, I'm more than happy to ask Vance to take you to the hotel because you're completely embarrassing me so far."

Daven was equally indignant now, but for entirely different reasons. "Did you even notice that his guards are carrying like five guns a piece? And there are four guards for one person, and only two of ours for *three* of us?"

"Of course I did! It's a power play. That's Harmon in a nutshell. If you can't handle it, just go and I'll manage this alone. I mean, what do you think is going to happen? They're going to start a shootout in the middle of a restaurant and assassinate us? This isn't the mafia, Dav, and we aren't mortal enemies. Settle down."

Daven didn't look remotely convinced, and indeed, he wasn't. "Fine. But we're not staying at the hotel Harmon recommended. I mean it, Hank. I'm putting my foot down."

Hank blinked, realizing that was actually a reasonable demand, which calmed him. "Okay. If that's what it's going to take for you to relax-"

"That, and you not telling him where we're really staying."

Hank was tired, and he didn't want to fight with Dav again. They had barely recovered from the last blowout, after all.

"*Fine*," Hank relented. "You pick the hotel, then. Don't tell me. If I don't know what it is, I can't possibly tell Harmon, can I?"

Daven hesitated, then agreed with a quick nod.

"Go coordinate with Theo, *discreetly*. Then get your ass back upstairs and behave yourself, or we're going to be having a very difficult conversation on the way home tomorrow."

"Yes, *sir*," Daven fired back bitterly. He hated being talked to like a bratty teenager, and thankfully Hank caught his error instantly.

"Sorry, Dav," he added hastily. "I'm...I should have phrased that differently."

Daven took a deep breath, then replied steadily, "Yes. But you're right, I need to calm down."

"Please do. We'll get through this as long as we stick together. Okay?" Hank clapped him on the shoulder and ran back up the stairs, realizing as he sat back down that he still had to piss. Badly. *Fuck.*

"Sorry, didn't mean to leave you sitting alone."

"That's alright. You done ripping Daven a new one?"

"What do you mean?" Hank lifted his huge wine glass and took a long swig to hide his expression. So much for hoping Harmon couldn't read him as well as he thought he could.

Harmon smirked slightly but didn't press the issue, thankfully. "I'm glad to see you two are on speaking terms again," he replied simply. "I'm still battling on that front with Colbert. Good man, really smart, but he rubs me the wrong way on an hourly basis."

"Hmm," Hank replied noncommittally, thankful for the distraction of his phone jangling loudly. It was Floyd, so he sent it to voicemail and then shut off the ringer.

"Sorry, forgot that was on. Listen, I regret this meeting got off to a rough start. Daven doesn't care for the manner in which your guards are armed, and I have to admit that I share the same concern. It's a bit unsettling."

Harmon actually laughed at that. "Ah. I see. Well, to each his own. You haven't been attacked. I have."

"I know."

"Not that I'm afraid of *you*, by any means. But San Diego isn't exactly an Urbane town."

"I know," Hank repeated, feeling suddenly ashamed of having mentioned the guards at all. Harmon had been attacked and nearly killed at a restaurant just down the street almost two years ago by a rogue extremist claiming to be from Hank's own party. Of course Harmon would be worried for his safety, and rightly so. *Smooth move, Hank...you daft idiot.*

Daven came back in the room, thankfully, and Harmon paid him no attention as he seated himself again.

"Hank, I'm under no illusions that this is going to be an easy discussion. Part of me...most of me...doesn't even want to be here right now. I want us to start off by you telling me exactly what led you to flip out on me last Saturday. You said you received a phone call?"

Hank glanced at Daven, who was calm again and wearing a blank expression.

"I did. One that I probably should have shared with Stewart, but we can debate that later."

"Okay. And?"

Hank hesitated and took a few sips of wine. "I know you're aware that I was accused of trying to bribe some photographers. They were all Urbanes, and I had given them a secondary number of mine to call. Anyway, moot point now, but on Saturday a man called me and said…"

He paused for some time as two ladies appeared with the appetizers and more wine was poured.

When they left, Harmon said with a small smile, "Don't stop now, you've got me on tenterhooks."

Hank swallowed hard. Nobody touched the food yet. "He said he got my number from one of those photographers. He knew about our planned meeting in Las Vegas, and told me not to trust you."

"Okay. Which you already don't. Then what?"

"Then…" Hank snuck another peek at Daven, who seemed unperturbed by what was said so far. "Well, first he offered to give me the name of someone in the government who could push through one of my measures. For a price, of course."

"Which one?"

"It...it's not relevant. I'm getting to the important part." Hank took a very deep breath, knowing there would be no turning back after this. "He said he works for you, and that he wants me to pay him for insider information so he can leave politics for a new life. He's not an Seditionist, either. Hates both of us."

Harmon flushed and set down his wine glass. "Well. Fuck."

"Yeah."

"Did you get his number, by chance?"

Hank nodded.

"Okay. What do I have to do in order to get that number? Speak plainly."

Hank reached into his pocket. "Nothing. It's right here." He handed him a slip of paper with the number, then held his breath until he was quite dizzy from the stress of giving over valuable information without getting anything in return.

Harmon looked at it for a long time, but there was no recognition. At least not any visible signs.

He set it down, then reached over to the appetizers. His countenance was suddenly grumpy and very typically Harmon.

"Alright, Hank. What are you playing at this time?" he asked somewhat rudely.

Hank gulped the last of his wine. "Excuse me?"

Daven put in, "He's not *playing* at anything. What are you implying?"

"Dav," Hank muttered, then to Harmon he replied steadily, "I just wanted to give you a show of good faith to prove that I'm serious about us establishing a cooperative and mutually beneficial relationship."

"It's definitely a *show,* for sure. This could be completely fabricated to trap me into something, and knowing you, I would most likely bet on it."

Hank raised his eyebrows, then calmly helped himself to some calamari. It was just as likely that Harmon was trying to entrap *him* with the call, but he didn't say that out loud.

"Well, you were right that this wasn't going to be an easy discussion."

Daven was all but writhing in his chair, and Hank threw him another *settle down* look.

Harmon chuckled a little. "But if not, I have a traitor in my midst, eh? Big shocker."

"You should be able to narrow it down easily enough," Daven mused thoughtfully, wisely heeding Hank's unspoken warning. "How many people knew about the meeting in Las Vegas?"

Hank was shocked when Harmon laughed again.

"This fellow who called you may not be as connected to me as he seems. My assistant, who has since been replaced, accidentally sent a company-wide email about the meeting, and I have 415 employees. Any single one of them could have told anybody in the world. But I assume you already knew that."

Well, shit, thought Hank. So much for impressing him with an intelligence freebie.

"I didn't know," he replied in a normal tone, fighting back the angry defensiveness that was shoving its way to the forefront of his mood. "But now you have a phone number to go on, at least."

"True. Thank you for that. I didn't mean to sound ungrateful."

"No problem," Hank answered gloomily. "Anyway, his rather frantic insistence that I not trust you or meet with you set me off. I sincerely apologize for that email I sent afterwards. My rudeness was uncalled for."

"Understood and forgiven."

"Thank you."

The conversation halted for several minutes as they all sampled the food, although Hank's appetite was long gone and he had to force himself to pretend to be enjoying it.

"What measure?" Harmon eventually asked, breaking the silence abruptly.

"What?"

"What measure did he offer to help you with? The government contact, I mean?"

"Oh. I've been trying for years to introduce legislation to make it illegal to profit off photos of minors. He wanted me to pay him for an introduction to someone who would help push it through. I have to admit that I seriously considered it for a minute."

Harmon refilled Hank's wineglass for him as he spoke. "Yeah, don't do that. Seriously illegal. Colton Gamble is who he meant. I will introduce you two by email tomorrow." He winked cheekily at Daven. "For free."

Daven was nearly as astonished as his boss at this unexpected generosity. "Why?" he asked suspiciously.

"Because such a law would also benefit my son, of course. Floyd and Theo aren't the only ones being harassed by those vultures. Hell, I'll back it myself, too. You should have come to me sooner, Hank."

"Thank you," Hank responded blandly, feeling out of sorts by the way Harmon was completely dominating the discussion and making him feel like a misguided child.

"Speaking of vultures," Harmon continued pleasantly, "I'm curious why you didn't invite Rupert to this dinner."

Hank flushed hotly at the reminder that there was no one who hated Harmon more than Rupert, and the feeling was unequivocally mutual. In fact, it was exactly like how Colbert hated Hank, and vice versa.

"I would assume for exactly same reasons you didn't bring Colbert," Hank replied politely.

"Ah. Touché."

Harmon was enjoying himself far too much; probably because his incessant ping-ponging between friendliness and contempt and back was making the other two men twitchy. Daven cleared his throat abruptly, and Hank idly noticed he hadn't touched his own wine. Smart man.

"Something on your mind, Daven?" asked Harmon with a completely straight face.

"Yes. Hank's mystery caller apparently knows Colton Gamble. Does that help narrow down his possible identity any further?"

It was an excellent question, and Hank was annoyed at himself for not thinking of it first. He was too busy being distracted by Harmon's jabs.

"Hardly," Harmon replied sullenly. "Colton was one of my employees for five years. Very popular. Left about a year ago, and I've had very few new hires since then. A handful, at the most."

Well, shit ...again.

"So now that we've had an exchange of valuable information, we're even," Harmon continued casually. "We got off to a good start, as agreed, so now it's time for the more difficult part of the discussion."

A good start. Hardly. Hank gulped again, but this time it was water. "Very well. Anything in particular?"

"Yes. I want to know what it will take for you to stop throwing me under the bus at every available opportunity. I know perfectly well how you forced me into my final warning with the FBI. That really was some exquisite orchestration, Hank. My congratulations to your success." He raised his glass in a mock toast.

Hank flinched, but forced himself to stay utterly diplomatic. "That was never my intention."

"Sure. The second thing I want to discuss is how to get you to agree to recall all of your double agents. Permanently."

Daven looked ready to pass out from the strain caused by this sudden change in direction. Fortunately nobody could say anything for several minutes as the main courses arrived and plates laid down and cleared away.

When the room was quiet again, Hank spoke up. "On the first point, if it's an apology you're looking for, I'm afraid you're going to be rather disappointed. I did what I had to do in order to protect the integrity of the investigation into Janet's murder."

"Of course you did," Harmon replied pleasantly. Too pleasantly.

Way too pleasantly.

"Hank," said Daven suddenly, sounding a bit strangled. "May we speak in private for a moment?"

Hank looked at Harmon, who nodded slyly, and the two friends got up and left the room again.

"Hank-"

"Hang on, I seriously have to piss. Just give me a second."

"Okay. I'll just wait here, then."

When Hank re-emerged, they went back into the empty storage room.

"Hank, I was right. This meeting was a mistake. He's making you look like a fool."

"Oh, thanks a lot. Appreciate that."

Dav met Hank's eyes, searching for any trace of mischief or humor in them, and found none.

"Dav, he's practically begging for a truce. He knows he's fucked with me working against him. We could take massive advantage of this. I'll say yes - make him grovel for it first, though - and then use this favor as leverage in the future to force him into cooperation on bigger matters."

Dav felt a little sick. "Sounds like the old diabolical Hank. You're trying to not be that person anymore, remember?"

"Think about it. The leverage we would have!"

"I *am* thinking about it. This is *Harmon* we're talking about. His only concern is protecting himself. And you're literally letting him get away with murder if you agree to not push back on the Janet investigation. He must be caught and punished, Hank, or else you're seriously disgracing her memory to help advance your own interests."

Hank was shocked and hurt by this callous assessment of his intentions. " *Our* interests. And 'disgracing her memory,' Dav, seriously? It's completely unfair to place all that on my shoulders, especially after I fought so hard for justice!"

Justice . Daven still had serious reservations about the whole debacle, but he dared not reopen that old wound. So he said nothing, which to Hank was far more telling than an actual reply.

"Okay, let's not go there again. But you're still for getting rid of our double agents, correct?"

"As much as I hate to side with Harmon on anything, yes I am."

"Okay. I trust you feel that way for a very good reason, and I'll tell him that I'll seriously consider it, but it's not going to happen. You know that, right?"

"So you're just making that decision now, without any further discussion?"

Hank held firm, even knowing he was breaking his own promise not to make big decisions without the input of Dav and Rupe. "Yes. Are you going to be able to live with that?"

Dav nodded, but his chest felt tight. "Not happy about it, but you're the boss."

"Is that a yes, or a no?"

"Yes, I can live with it."

"Good. Thank you. There's one more thing, and I don't want you to read into it or get all flustered. When we're wrapping up this meeting, I will ask you to go downstairs and have Vance pull the car around. Just go, without argument. Okay?"

Dav suddenly looked as dismayed as a cat being forcibly bathed, and Hank suppressed a frustrated sigh.

"Why? You...you *want* to be alone with him?"

"Just for a minute. There's something I have to tell him that's highly confidential. Just do it. Okay?"

Dav shrugged. "Obviously I have no choice."

CHAPTER FOUR

The second half of the dinner was similar to the first half, and Hank was becoming thoroughly worn out by his complete inability to read Harmon. He considered himself a master people reader and therefore wasn't used to this situation, nor was he used to anyone being able to read himself as annoyingly accurate as Harmon could.

It was incredibly strange that they had the opposite experience with each other over the phone, where Hank always had the upper hand and could correctly anticipate Harmon's every response. In person, however, he felt utterly blindfolded and clumsy. It wasn't like this back when they were last together in Philadelphia a few weeks ago, nor the time before that.

How the tables had turned, and Hank had no clue why that was.

Soon after dessert was finished - probably too soon - Hank decided to call it a night, citing their extremely early departure time back to Los Angeles.

"Daven, will you kindly go ask Vance to pull the car around? I'll be down in a minute."

"Yes, sir," he replied formally, to Hank's quiet relief, and all three men stood up at the same time. Harmon was the first to extend his hand.

"Good to see you again, Daven. Until next time."

"Safe travels."

Then he was gone, and Harmon turned to his rival with an audible sigh.

"Having that man in the same room increases my blood pressure by about 30 points. Does he have that same effect on you?"

Hank shook his head. "Quite the opposite, actually. That's why I insisted he be here."

They sat back down, and the old Harmon Hank was used to suddenly revealed himself.

"So. That conversation was more difficult than I anticipated. But I think we found common ground on a few surprising points, and no surprises on those things we've always disagreed about and will continue to clash over."

Hank took a deep breath, steeling himself for what he was about to ask.

"Right. Uh, there was one subject I didn't bring up because it's rather testy. Daven and I have clashed on it a number of times before. Are you aware that our government is planning to bring back public flogging?"

"Yes."

"May I ask how you feel about it?"

"Against it, as you are."

Hank was confused for a moment. "How did you know I was against it?"

"I wouldn't expect anything less. But that's not even the worst of my worries. Are you aware that it's been proposed that indentured minors should be castrated at age 16, and muted at the first sign of dissidence after age 18?"

Hank gasped, feeling truly sick to his stomach suddenly. "What? No. Holy fuck. What kind of country are we becoming? When did this come up?"

"Yesterday. You really need to join the public policy briefing calls once in a while."

Hank took another huge swig of the wine he'd been avoiding for the past hour.

"I will from now on. Rupert always does them, but we haven't connected in a couple days."

Harmon shrugged. "Might want to hurry. The measures will probably be on the March 1 ballot. You know as well as I do that once something passes, we can't touch it with a hundred-mile pole. If you want to work together on those two new issues, I will, but I'm not stupid or reckless enough to dare protest what is already law, so we have to move fast."

Indeed, even openly discussing fighting a passed law was nearly treason in itself, and it was deeply ingrained within both men that such matters were utterly beyond their control for ten years, after which new measures could be proposed to replace them. After all, the laws had been passed with the votes of their very own constituents in the first place. If things went south, the failure lay on their own shoulders for not leading their parties in the right direction.

"Well," Hank said, sweating a little, "Yes, I absolutely want to work together with you on it. But I might have a slight problem. Daven and Rupert don't feel the same way I do about such matters. And you know that my constituents overwhelmingly favor more severe measures for criminals than I do. Than *we* do, rather."

Harmon nodded. "Yes, I know, and that's why I'm continually surprised that your super delegates keep electing you."

That wasn't meant as an insult or a slight, Hank knew. It was simply the truth. He thought for sure he would never be elected again after several ugly, public feuds with his delegates - and even his own executives - over the more severe indentured servitude measures. But somehow, he was still here and more popular than ever. It defied logic.

"So...are you saying you want to work with me even against the wishes of your chief of staff and PR guy?"

Hank shook his head. "Of course not. I would prefer to try and align them with me. If I can't do that...I don't know what to do then. I can all but guarantee there's going to be a huge fight.

My constituents can be huge assholes. So can my executives.
Lately I feel like...like I'm leading the wrong party, to be
honest."

He stopped himself cold, not even being able to register the
horrible words from his own mouth. While that's exactly how
he'd felt for several months since the October 1994 vote had
gone awry, he certainly had not meant to admit such a thing to
anybody. He'd barely even accepted it himself, so why the hell
did he just blurt it out to *Harmon,* of all people?

Jesus fucking Christ...

Harmon must have been incredibly surprised by such an
admission, but he didn't change expression at all. "I'll pretend
I didn't hear that. I know what you really meant. I clash with
my own constituents sometimes, too."

Hank stood up, heart pounding. "Fuck. Too much wine," he
lamely declared. "I need to go. The bill is paid, right?"

"Yes. Just relax."

"This dinner was a mistake. This meeting. We're never doing it
again."

"Hank, don't panic. I know what you meant. I'm not going to-"

Holy fuck, Hank whispered to himself as he left the room abruptly and all but flew down the stairs to the safety of his entourage.

"Which car is Daven in?" he asked Avery, who was waiting stiffly at the exit.

"The front car."

Hank got in the rear car, where Theo was sound asleep on the front bench. He climbed over him and into the back row, noting that Harmon's five guards were all out front, watching the party's departure closely and with some apparent amusement.

"Let's go, Vance. Quickly, but don't peel out."

"Yes, sir."

"Everything go okay, boss? A little concerned about this hurried departure."

"Uh, yeah. Thanks Avery. I just realized how late it was getting, that's all."

Hank went to take off his tie, but his hands were trembling too much to manage, so he gave up and leaned back with his eyes closed, trying to breathe again. Avery was watching him through the mirror, but Hank couldn't see the deep concern and alarm on the man's face.

Your transparency will be the death of you, Hank...

CHAPTER FIVE

On the way to Carlsbad, same evening.

"Sorry, dad," Theo said sleepily as the car pulled onto the freeway with a lurch.

Hank opened his eyes to find Theo peering cautiously through the headrest at him.

"Sorry for what?"

"Stealing your seat."

"Don't be silly. Where are we staying, anyway? Do you have your seatbelt on?"

"Yeah. The Omni in Carlsbad."

"Good. Nice place. As soon as we get upstairs I want you in bed."

"So...we're not having a *chat,* then?"

Hank was so wildly distracted and depressed that he couldn't even recall what his son had done wrong, and he wasn't about to ask.

"No. You're forgiven."

Theo's surprise and relief was palpable, and he melted into the words and laid his chin on the seat, looking backwards at his dad with curious, wide eyes. "Thank you. Are you okay?"

"Yup. Just a little too much wine making me queasy."

"Gross. Don't barf on me, dad."

Now Hank smiled as he reached out to ruffle Theo's mop of hair. "I won't. Did you enjoy your dinner?"

"Yeah, and Vance let me have a bite of his cake."

Hank eyed his driver in the rearview mirror. Normally the man's semi-horrified expression would make him laugh, but not now. Nothing on earth could make him laugh at the moment.

"It's not nice to tattle, Theo."

"Just being honest."

"No, you're being a tattle-tale. Don't be that."

"Okay, sorry. Oh I forgot to tell you, Floyd tried to call you but I told him you were busy. He wants us to call him at six on Friday."

Now he had Hank's full attention. "You didn't tell him who we were with, did you?"

"Of course not, dad. I'm not a tattle-tale."

Hank grinned. "Of course not." He saw Theo shiver and immediately took off his own jacket. "Here, put this over you. Vance, can you turn down the a/c a bit? It's January, you know."

"Sorry, sir. About the cake, too."

"No harm done."

Theo laid back down and was soon asleep again. They arrived at the hotel about twenty minutes later, and Hank climbed back out over his youngest, poking him as he went.

"Hey, you're too old to carry. Up."

Theo didn't respond, so Avery reached in and lifted him out, still partially covered in Hank's jacket. Daven then appeared, dutifully rolling his little royal blue suitcase that went everywhere with him. He silently followed Hank and Avery to the elevator, obviously hoping to hear how the meeting ended.

"Thanks, Dav. You did good tonight," Hank said graciously after the elevator doors closed.

"You, too. Your restraint was...admirable."

Admirable, indeed. Up until the last 30 seconds, anyway.

"And exhausting. We'll talk tomorrow on the way home."

Hank always insisted on connecting rooms to their guards, and was relieved to see that Theo had arranged for exactly that even though he forgot to mention it. Of course. He was a good kid, and smart.

Avery carried Theo to the bed and covered him up just as Hank collapsed into his own bed.

"Aren't you going to tuck me in too, Avery? Tell me a bedtime story?"

The big man grinned. "There once was a man from Nantucket, who told the big boss to go f-"

"Alright, alright. Forget it. Go to bed."

Avery laughed and disappeared into his room.

Despite Hank's exhaustion and the effects of the wine, he never managed to fall asleep.

There was so much to think about and do before the March 1 vote. He couldn't believe such drastic, draconian measures would actually pass. But then again, his constituents were pretty harsh on criminal behavior. They could afford to be, what with being mostly affluent; nearly all upper and upper-middle class. People like that didn't care about the welfare of lawbreakers and the disadvantaged. It was Harmon's party who probably wouldn't support the laws - almost certainly wouldn't - and Hank took a brief moment to pray that for once the man's greater number of constituents could outvote his own. That happened rarely, but it wasn't so uncommon that it was impossible.

The problem was that a good ten percent of the nation's citizens were independent, unaffiliated voters of all walks of life. They usually sided with the Seditionists because of Hank's popularity and clean-cut reputation. Almost *always* sided with them, in fact. While that could be a good thing when Hank wanted certain laws passed, it was the opposite when he was personally against his own constituent's wishes. And that's where things could - and had - gone seriously wrong. In fact, since the previous May, the independents had been voting for all the measures he didn't support, at least privately. But he supported them publicly, because that's what his constituents wanted. That's what he was elected for. He had to do his job. Had to speak the words written for him to fight for laws he didn't want.

Hank Bancroft was a conflicted man, and his secret hypocrisy was wearing him thin. After nine years in this position, and especially with increasingly harsh measures passed against people who couldn't fight back, his bleeding liberal heart had started to beat strongly again. And if these March 1 laws went through, it couldn't be ignored any longer.

Then again, it was probably already starting to show itself. He hadn't been kind to Daven and Rupert since the October vote; in fact he hadn't been himself ever since last summer, when they first showed their support of deeply conservative measures that he didn't expect them to ever consider. It was then that he had begun quietly turning against his own constituents. Against his own party.

He hadn't told anybody that, of course. Until tonight. And then he told the worst person possible.

 For the vast majority of citizens, the system worked and the laws were inherently good - free healthcare for all and mandatory mental health facilities and homeless shelters in every town over a certain population being a good example of many. That was because they all voted for these things - *all* of them, and that was Hank's doing.

He was very proud of the one passed measure he had personally written and introduced. Because low voter turnout had resulted in the disastrous Durdan presidency that led to the Second American Revolution, citizens 19 years and older of The Reunited States were now required to vote by phone on major laws on the first of every month, except January. Implementing the intricate voice recognition technology had cost a bloody fortune, but it worked incredibly well. Those who did not vote without being excused were heavily fined and sentenced to 100 hours of community service. So far, less than one percent of the population had been noncompliant, which meant 99% of the nation phoned in 6 times a year to vote. It was rather astonishing when compared to the dismal 12% turnout in November of 1980.

Mandatory voting had one major downside, and that was the effect of inequality in social status on passing laws. Convicted criminals and Bonded Retainers could not vote at all, for life - no matter how long they had been free or what their crimes were, and they were a significant population. This resulted in a law that prohibited appeals in death sentence cases. Fifteen years ago, before Reunification, those appeals were automatic, but citizens had become tired of paying for criminals to live on death row for 50 years. They had jumped at the chance to change it. Especially the Seditionists - who were not at all concerned with the welfare of such individuals. Hank was thoroughly ashamed of backing that measure, but he would have been mutinied out of office if he didn't. So his popularity grew as "Death Row" was phased out and executions became mandatory within 7 days of the sentence.

Another law he opposed was the one that prohibited day laborers coming from across the border in Mexico. As he had predicted, crucial farms and fields in Texas and the southwest states were soon plunged into dire straits due to lack of workers. A near-famine soon followed, but the law could not be repealed for ten years. Hence, the hasty introduction of indentured servitude for criminals more than a hundred years after it had been phased out after the Civil War. No one was proud of the arrangement, and it was little better than slavery, but it worked to feed the country again. Convicted men and women could choose "service," or prison. They almost always chose indenture, which by unintended consequence had already fixed the prison overpopulation problems that had plagued the nation ever since the War on Drugs had begun. In fact, it had put the much-despised private prison industry out of business completely.

Again, Hank's popularity wildly increased as he mourned the win.

But then the slippery slope got greased even more, the nation lost its compassionate side over time, and it soon got proposed that children of convicted felons also became indentured. Despite the fact that Hank *and* Harmon had firmly and publicly opposed it, the measure passed in October. Both of them had a brief but massive downturn in popularity for that.

Some things you just couldn't control.

Hank turned around on his side and watched Theo sleep for a while, and by the time his 4:30am alarm went off, he already knew he wouldn't be running for reelection this fall. He had enough money to live off already without ever having to work again, and he already had bought floor plans for a big cabin on a lake near Yosemite for retirement.

Why wait until then?

So that was that. The decision calmed him, and he woke Theo up with a smile on his face and a lightness in his heart that he hadn't felt for almost a year.

"Daven," said Avery quietly as they waited in the car for Hank to appear at the valet stand with Lucas. "I wanted to ask...I mean, is Hank alright? I was really worried about him last night, and I haven't seen him this morning."

Dav cocked his head. "Why do you ask?"

"He didn't look well when he got in the car afterwards."

"Too much wine, I'm afraid. He usually only gets drunk once a year, on Christmas."

"I know, but it wasn't that. Panicked, more like. I almost asked if he'd seen a ghost. I'm sorry. It's none of my business. But if Harmon said or did something to him, I'm going to…I don't know what I'm going to do, but something."

Daven took in the words bitterly, but tried not to jump to conclusions. Now he really needed to know how the meeting ended. He was going to *demand* to know.

"You're right, it's none of your business, so you're not going to do anything about it."

Avery swallowed hard. He rarely talked to Daven, and that was exactly because the man had no problem being abrasive if he felt it was warranted. Like right now.

Jesus, what a dick. "Right. Sorry."

"No problem," Daven replied pleasantly. "If you can roll up the window after we pull away, I'll get to the bottom of it. Thank you for telling me."

Avery looked back at him in surprise. That was Daven, ice cold one moment and totally fine the next.

"Yes, sir."

"Don't call me sir."

Hank suddenly appeared and Dav was relieved to see him make his way back to Avery's SUV after ushering the still-sleepy Theo to the other car.

Daven was astonished to see him in a good mood as he jumped in and spread out in the front row with a big sigh.

"Good morning, Hank."

"Top o' the morning. Ouch. I shouldn't talk so loud. My head. Avery, can you pull through somewhere for breakfast? McDonald's or whatever."

"Yes, boss. Shall I roll up the privacy glass?"

"Not right now. Thanks. Dav, can you hand me the blue blanket in the very back row?"

"It's in the other car," replied Avery quickly as he opened his door. "I'll get it."

He was gone in a flash, and Daven seized the moment to question his boss. "How did the meeting end? Did you say whatever you wanted to say to Harmon?"

Hank nodded, but kept his eyes on Avery. "Yes, and we're fine. We're good."

Daven thought about Avery's description of him as *panicked*. "Hmmm. And he didn't...like, threaten you or anything? Or try to pull something while I was out of the room?"

"No, Dav. Everything's fine. Don't worry about it." Now he turned around to look at his friend. "Why are you so upset? You look like someone just ran over your dog."

"It's just...I couldn't help but notice you seemed a little alarmed afterwards. That's all. I just want to make sure you're okay."

Avery opened the door and handed the big cashmere blanket to Hank, who folded himself up in it and leaned against the window, grumbling to himself. Daven wasn't even in the same damned car last night, how could he know what...

Oh. Of course. Avery.

"Sorry, I'm really tired. Going to take a nap. We'll have to continue this later."

"Okay. But we should talk before we get back to the office."

"Hmm. We'll see."

"Did you not sleep well?" Daven pressed. "Was it something Harmon said?"

"For god's sake, Dav! Stop. I'm fine. Avery, did you forget how to drive?" he snapped.

"Sorry, boss." Avery looked straight at Daven as he turned around and quickly backed out of the driveway, raising his eyebrows slightly as if to say, *See? Told you so.*

Daven shrugged and picked up his Blackberry. There were at least two new messages from Rupert inquiring about the meeting, but he skipped over them both and went straight to the one with the subject: *Draft: Proposed Media Statement supporting the Public Flogging initiative.*

CHAPTER SIX

Thursday morning

Hank never managed to fall asleep in the car, either, but he stayed leaning against the window and kept his eyes closed in order to avoid conversation with Daven, who was catching up on his email with a deep frown on his face. He wasn't really worried at the moment about what had happened between Hank and Harmon in the final minute of their meeting. It was the draft media statement from Rupert that was bothering him. Thinking Hank was sound asleep, he asked Avery to roll up the privacy glass and then quietly picked up the phone and called Rupe as they passed through Marina del Rey on the office.

"It's Daven."

"Yes. I know. Caller ID, for the millionth time. Where are you guys?"

"About twenty minutes away from the office. Lucas is on the way to your house with Theo. I just read your draft statement and can tell you right now Hank's going to hate it."

Pause. "Can you be more specific?"

"Well, for one thing, he's totally against this measure. The draft makes it sounds like he's all but gleeful to be supporting it."

"I know, but that's the job. And he's the only one who's against it."

"That doesn't matter, Rupe. He's the boss."

"Right you are, but he doesn't make *those* decisions. Our constituents do. Our delegates do. He's going to have to suck it up."

Daven sighed. "Rupe, you didn't copy him on the draft and I'm assuming that's because you don't want to fight. But that's exactly what's going to happen. Tone it down and resend it, and copy him."

"Excuse me? You're not my boss, Daven, so don't order me around. I'll speak to Hank directly when you guys get here."

"I'm just trying to prevent-"

The line disconnected and Daven all but threw down his phone in frustration, not noticing that Hank was watching him curiously.

"Did Rupe just hang up on you?" he asked after a moment, and Daven jumped.

"I'm so sorry, Hank. Did I wake you?"

"Nope. What's going on?"

Daven explained the conversation, and Hank's expression darkened. On one hand, it was great to know that Dav was maybe starting to sway to his side regarding the public flogging issue. That was unexpected. On the other hand, now he had to deal with an argument between two men who had never argued before, at least not to his knowledge. Perhaps it was just a one-time thing. He hoped, anyway. It was the last thing he needed right now.

"Okay, sorry Dav. Totally unacceptable for him to hang up on you. I'll deal with that. You just carry on as normal."

"I can handle it, Hank."

"I'm his boss, it's my responsibility. Just because we're all friends doesn't mean-"

He stopped talking in surprise as Avery rolled down the privacy glass all the way.

"Sir, we're getting pulled over. Roll down your windows."

That was law when a car had tinted windows, so Daven and Hank immediately complied on both sides of the car.

"What happened?" Hank asked as he reached all the way over to the passenger side.

"I changed lanes without signaling."

Hank said nothing, although his irritation almost made a rude comeback irresistible.

The police officer cautiously approached the car and peered into the back seats.

"Good morning, officer," Daven and Hank said together.

"Good morning Mr. Bancroft, Mr. Johansson."

He proceeded to Avery. "You changed lanes without signaling, son. Right in front of me, too. What's the deal?"

"The man on the blue motorcycle, sir. I thought he was going to veer into my lane. I was wrong."

While this discussion was taking place Hank had of course noticed two photographers across the street taking pictures of the scene, and all but prayed the officer would issue a ticket so there wouldn't have to be an argument about it.

"Alright. I saw him too, he was all over the place. So I'm going to let it slide this time."

"Officer," said Hank quickly from his spot next to the window. "Please issue the ticket anyway, or else I'm going to be nailed in the press for acting like I'm above the law."

"You kind of are, sir," said the officer with a small smile. "I'll get in a heap of trouble if I ticket you."

Hank swallowed hard. That shouldn't be true, but it was. "But...you'd be citing him, not me. Please just do it."

The officer shook his head and tucked his ticketing pad back into his jacket. "An honor to meet you, Mr. Bancroft. Mr. Johansson. Have a nice day."

He went back to his car and sped off in the opposite direction, and it took the rest of the drive to the office for Hank's heart to slow back down to normal again. He already could picture the scathing headlines the next day in the paper's political section.

Damned if you do, damned if you don't.

"I'm really sorry about that, sir," said Avery after Daven got out of the car when they arrived at the office. "But I figure the press would be a hell of a lot worse for you if we killed somebody."

"It certainly would," Hank mused. "Thank you for putting it into perspective." He aborted his attempt to exit and stayed in the car, leaving Daven looking at him in confusion as the door shut again. "And I'm sorry for barking at you earlier today when we left the hotel. But I need to ask you something. Did you tell Daven I was acting strange after the dinner ended last night?"

Now it was Avery's turn to swallow hard. "I didn't use the word strange, sir. I said...that you looked unwell and I was concerned for you."

"Is that all?"

"I think...I think I used the word *panicked* ."

"Okay. That explains a lot." Hank glanced out at Daven, who was still standing there waiting for him. "Avery, I'm only going to say this once, and I mean it. If you *ever* do that again, you're off my team. You have a problem with me, or any concerns, you ask me directly. What you said to Daven is going to cause a problem between me and him. I know you meant well, but never again. Understand?"

The huge man looked about ready to cry, and Hank pushed aside the instinct to feel bad about being so harsh. He was absolutely right, and he wasn't going to back down.

"Yes, sir. Understood. I only asked him because he cares about you just as much as I do. There was no harm intended at all."

"I know. But you have a duty of confidentiality to me." To drive the message home even further, he took the man off duty for the day. That would sting worse than any words could. "Go home, and send Brittany back to pick me up at noon."

He got out of the car before Avery could answer and rejoined Daven. "I'm going to cut the day short, but we need to talk for a few minutes. Your office. I'll meet you there in ten minutes."

He headed to the cafeteria and got some coffee and a bagel, and headed back upstairs with a heavy heart. There was nothing more he hated than conflicts with his friends, and it hurt him to know that Rupert had treated Daven so poorly this morning.

Daven was waiting by the window in his office, and Hank walked in and shut the door behind him.

"Dav, I just had it out with Avery for telling you I was panicked when we left the restaurant last night. He knows better than that. I'm sorry he upset you for nothing."

"So he was wrong?"

"I wasn't panicked," Hank said, taking a huge bite of his bagel. It took a minute to get it down his throat so he could continue, but that allowed him more time to think. "Harmon pisses me off. I was angry that he was enjoying toying with us. You commended me on my restraint but I don't feel like I should have been so restrained. We looked weak."

Daven shook his head. "I disagree. No offense, but you look awful. You should go home."

"I haven't slept."

"I can tell."

"I need to deal with Rupert first, then the auditors. After that I'm gone. Where's the draft of the media statement?"

Daven wordlessly handed him a printed sheet of paper, and Hank looked around for the big fluffy chair to collapse into. *Oh...it's gone. That's right.* He settled into the ugly modern couch instead, and drank down the rest of his coffee as he read the statement. Daven was right. He hated it.

"Okay, this sucks. Look, I know we've clashed over this topic before. But let's put that aside."

"As I said earlier, I'm changing my mind about it. You should know that Rupert strongly supports it, though, and I don't even need to mention that all the delegates are highly enthused about it." He shuddered. "Public flogging. What a way to set our country back 150 years."

"You mean 23 years. You won't believe this, but it actually wasn't banished in Delaware until 1972, although the last incident took place in 1952. I've studied this topic way too much. There's a reason we outlawed it the first time. At least Harmon learns from history; he said he's going to oppose it."

Daven shrugged. "I wouldn't expect anything else. His constituents would drag him out of office kicking and screaming if he supported it."

Hank grimaced. "You mean like ours will with me, if I speak against it?"

Dav nodded, his face just as grave.

"Fuck," Hank sighed as he tossed the paper on the coffee table and laid down on the couch. "I don't even care, Dav. Let them."

"Hank. You really need to get some sleep before you talk yourself into walking off the job."

Too late…

"Hang on." He sat up and took his vibrating phone out of his pocket. It was Floyd's school again.

"Hank Bancroft."

"Mr. Bancroft, Silas Rawson here. Floyd's fine, don't be alarmed."

Don't be alarmed? Seriously? "Okay. What's going on?"

"He didn't show up for class this morning so I went to check on him and he was packing up all his stuff. Wants to go home, and I'm afraid he's rather dead set on it."

"That sounds like anything but *fine* to me. I take it he's in his room now?"

"Yes, sir."

"I'll call him. Thanks." He hung up and turned to his chief of staff. "I got to go to my office, Dav. I'll let you know when I'm done dealing with Rupert."

Hank trudged to his office and shut the door, paying no attention to the line of people waiting outside to have a word with him.

Floyd picked up on the first ring. "Dad?"

"Floyd, what in the holy hell are you up to now? You're not leaving, so forget it and go back to class."

"Dad, please. I hate it here!"

Hank acted astonished, though he was far from it. "What? Why?"

"Because Theo's not here. Because you're not here. I hate it. I have no friends."

"You've been there *four days*. Give it time."

"This was a mistake. You let me choose to come here, so why won't you let me choose to leave?"

Floyd had a good point, that much was certain. And if he was totally honest with himself, Hank knew this was going to happen all along. Counted on it, actually.

"Alright son, listen up. Four days is not enough to fix everything that's been wrong in the past three months. You're going to stay there, and you're going to shape up, and-"

"Dad!"

"-and if I get one more call about you skipping class-"

"Dad, please," Floyd pleaded, the words issuing forth in a rapid tumble. "I'm miserable. I haven't eaten in two days, my stomach is killing me, this is the wrong place for me. I'm in the wrong school, with the wrong people, everything is just wrong. I quit. I'll be good, I promise. Please come get me. I'll never give you a reason to be mad at me again, I swear. Whatever you want."

"Floyd, you can't quit. It's not a job." Hank breathed deeply, suddenly feeling completely sympathetic for his oldest now that he heard the tears catching in the poor boy's throat. If anyone knew what it was like to be in the wrong place with the wrong crowd, it was Hank Bancroft.

There was silence on the other end of the line for a long time, during which Hank hit the concealed button on his desk to summon Dav. That was how he sometimes got out of meetings that went on too long, and he thought it was sly but the whole office had caught on to the tactic a long time ago.

"You still there, kiddo?"

"Yeah, dad. I miss you," he said softly.

Well, so much for Hank's resolve. Poof. Gone.

"Miss me? I thought you hated me lately. And Theo."

"I thought I did, too, but I don't. I'm sorry I've been a di...that I've been acting up so much. I'll never do it again, I swear."

Daven peeked through the window and Hank crooked his finger to signal him to enter.

"Floyd, hold on for a minute. Just...don't hang up. Hold on."

Hank put his son on mute. "Close the door. Dav, I have a really awkward favor to ask you. Feel free to say no."

"Okay. What?"

"You don't have any meetings today, right?"

"No."

"Can you and Lucas go get Floyd from school in Palm Springs? You're listed as his second guardian so they'll release him to you, but not to my guards. I'm too fucking tired, and I've got that mandatory 11am meeting with the auditors from the FBI."

Daven was instantly concerned. "Sure. Is everything alright?"

"Yeah. Poor kid is homesick. You guys will have to take the Escalade so there's room for all his suitcases."

"Sure. Leave right now?"

"Yeah, if that's ok. It'll take about three hours each way."

Daven nodded. "Sure, Hank. Anything for Floyd."

Hank felt a catch in his throat suddenly, and his heart was all but glowing. "You're a good man, Dav. I'm...thankful for your friendship. And for caring about Floyd. Thank you."

Dav nodded, again. "Are you alright?"

"Yeah," Hank said with a smile. "Getting my boy back when I thought I was going to lose him? Everything's great. I'm going to let you surprise him with the good news. Hurry back, alright?"

"Certainly. See you at the house."

Hank picked up the phone again. "Hey, Floyd. I'm going into a meeting and I want you to just relax and breathe. Do your meditations. Take your medications. Do what you got to do to chill out, okay? We'll talk later about possibly bringing you home at spring break. I can't promise anything."

"*Spring break?*" Floyd moaned. "But I'm ready now, dad. I'm packed."

"Floyd. We will *only* talk if Silas can confirm for me that you went back to class right now and stayed there all three hours. Period. Otherwise, forget it, we aren't talking about a thing. Understood? Call me at lunchtime."

"Yes, sir," Floyd replied miserably, and Hank smiled a little himself.

"Good boy. Talk to you then."

He hung up and dialed Silas.

"Silas, I lost the bet. He lasted three days less than I thought he would. I'm really glad you talked me into paying only one week's tuition."

Silas laughed a little. "Oh, that's alright. He's a good kid. No harm done and we've enjoyed having him. So you're coming to pick him up?"

"No, my brother Daven is on his way." Hank stopped himself in surprise; he had never referred to Dav as his brother before and wasn't sure why he did so now. It was strange that it didn't feel awkward at all. "He and my guard, Lucas, should be there by noon or so. Don't tell Floyd. They're going to surprise him, but I want his ass back in class now until lunchtime. He knows, but can you make sure?"

"Of course."

Hank was happy as that call ended and another rough chapter in the book of Floyd was coming to an end. He missed his kid more than he'd ever confess, although he'd admittedly been too occupied to think about him much lately.

Now to deal with Rupert. He walked over to the man's office, once again ignoring the line of people waiting to talk to him. Normally he'd never be so rude, but this wasn't a normal day.

"Hank, welcome back," said Rupe as he pulled a piece of paper off his printer. "I was just about to bring you the revised version of the media st...is something wrong?"

Hank sat down at one of the chairs in front of the desk, which he never did. "First things first. As predicted, Floyd's time at Elite Palms has come to a premature end."

"No problem. Millie's ready for him. I'm glad the boys won't be separated anymore."

"Good. Thank you." Hank hardened his tone. "Now for the part where I get bitchy, and you shut up and listen, and then quickly agree to everything I expect to happen in the future."

Rupert's eyes went wide with alarm; Hank had never said such a ruthless thing to him before.

"Yes?"

"I overheard the conversation you had with Dav. Two big things wrong with it. Number one, if he tells you to do something, you do it. He's always done what you tell him without hesitation because he understands you both work for me, not yourselves. So don't let your pride get in the way of the job again. Got that?"

"Yes, Hank," Rupe replied quietly.

"Second thing. You hung up on him. Totally disrespectful and I won't have it. Have I ever hung up on you mid-sentence, even when I'm completely pissed off beyond all proportion to reality?"

"No, come to think of it."

"Exactly. Some lines we just don't cross, and that's one of them. You know that, we've discussed this before. I'll admit I did it once to Dav, but I spent a week apologizing for it. Next time it happens, you're out an entire paycheck. I'm dead serious."

"Understood, Hank," Rupert said placatingly. Hank was more furious than he'd since him since the Christmas debacle, but he was speaking in a near-conversational tone and was completely in control otherwise. It was terrifying somehow.

"Thank you. Then this matter is closed and won't be brought up again. Let me see that revised press release, please." He held his hand out, but Rupe froze.

"Hank, please let me say something first. I know that you're fundamentally against this law. After speaking to Daven I've changed the wording quite a bit, to make it much less...enthusiastic. But you must know that our party needs to support this." Hank nodded, so Rupe took a deep breath and handed over the new draft, which Hank read several times before commenting.

"Rupe, this is really good. It think you nailed it."

"What? Really?" Rupert did not expect that reaction. "I thought you...you.."

"No, you're right. Our party needs to support this. It's who we are. It doesn't matter that I'm personally against it." He handed the paper back. "Don't release it yet, though. I got word that the law might be on the March 1 ballot, so I'd like to wait a little longer before proceeding with an endorsement. Things change fast around here."

Rupert nodded. "Of course. That makes perfect sense."

"Hmm. Thanks again for taking Floyd into the home school. I'm leaving at noon because I didn't sleep last night. We'll catch up tomorrow."

Hank went back to his office and fired up his email program.

Harmon: how sure are you that this public flogging measure is going to be on the March 1 ballot? Need to know so we can align our messaging. Get back to me ASAP please. Hope you're enjoying the rest of your vacation. -Hank

Hank went into his bathroom to calm his nerves, and it took some time to get back to the point where he could be seen in public again without raising eyebrows. He must look terrible.

By the time he got back to his desk there was already a reply.

Hank, my contact says it's certain. I'm planning to release our statement around February 18. May I assume you will still be opposing it, and the others we discussed?

Oh shit, here goes, thought Hank. Into the belly of the beast we proceed.

Yes, exactly as discussed. Talk to you on Monday, 10am PST.

Hank felt sick, but he was committed now. If he couldn't persuade Rupert and Daven that opposing the two measures was best for the party, then fuck it. He was going to oppose them anyway with a live press conference before they could stop him, and damn the consequences.

He reached over and pulled the heavy carved stone paperweight into his lap, slowly and idly tracing the lettering with his fingers as he always did when he was uncertain about a decision. The quote always helped him settle down and re-center, and he always felt better afterwards:

There comes a time when one must take a position that is neither safe, nor politic, nor popular, but he must take it because conscience tells him it is right.